In a faraway land, where the sun scorches the fiery desert, there lies an ancient secret.

It is a lamp, long forgotten and buried deep beneath the shifting sands. It is small and simple. It bears no fancy design and contains no precious jewels. To all but the wisest among us, it would appear dull and worthless.

But this lamp is not what it seems. Long ago, it held the greatest power in all the lands of Arabia. Its magic changed for ever the course of a young man's life. A young man who, like the lamp, was more than he seemed.

The tale begins on a dark night, where a dark man, on a dark horse, waits with a dark purpose...

Ladybird books are widely available, but in case of difficulty may be ordered by post or telephone from:
Ladybird Books – Cash Sales Department Littlegate Road Paignton Devon TQ3 3BE Telephone 0803 554761

A catalogue record for this book is available from the British Library

Published by Ladybird Books Ltd Loughborough Leicestershire UK
LADYBIRD and the device of a Ladybird are trademarks of Ladybird Books Ltd

Disney

Aladdin

Ladybird

The man's name was Jafar. His beady eyes and pointed turban gave him the look of a cobra about to strike. A parrot, perched on his shoulder, cocked its head impatiently. Jafar's horse shifted beneath him and gave a restless snort. But the dark man was prepared to wait.

The treasure was buried somewhere out there. Only one person would be able to find it—the person who possessed both halves of an ancient scarab medallion. Jafar had one half, and soon he would have the other. Then the treasure would be his. And when it was, he would become the most powerful man in Agrabah.

In the stillness, Jafar heard the clopping of hooves as a rider approached.

The man was a common thief named Gazeem. He had agreed to bring Jafar the other half of the medallion in return for part of the treasure. Jafar had promised.

Jafar had lied!

"You are late," the dark man said.

Gazeem dismounted and bowed his head. Jafar was the Royal Vizier, the chief adviser to the Sultan. It was not wise to upset him. "My apologies, O Patient One," Gazeem said.

Jafar glared. "You have it, then?" he asked.

With a grin, the thief pulled the half medallion from his pocket.

Jafar reached for it, but the thief held it back. "What about the treasure? You promised me…"

SCREECH! The parrot swooped down from Jafar's shoulder, grabbed the medallion and dropped it into Jafar's bony hand.

"Trust me," Jafar said. "You'll get what's coming to you."

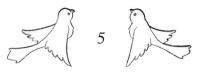

Quickly he took out his half of the medallion. He could feel his heart pounding as he fitted the halves together. They glowed. Then...

BOOOOOM! A clap of thunder shook the desert. The medallion leapt from Jafar's hand as if it were alive. It streaked across the dunes.

Jafar dug his spurs into his horse's sides. "Quickly, follow it!" he shouted.

Gazeem mounted his own horse and raced after Jafar. Bright as a comet, the medallion shot towards a small sandstone. It circled round it, then hovered in the air.

CRACK! The medallion split in two again and plunged into the rock, each half wedging into a small hole.

Jafar stopped his horse and jumped off. The pulsing halves of the medallion stared out at him like a huge pair of eyes. An exhilarating chill bolted through him. There was no turning back now.

RRRRROMMMMM! The earth began to tremble. The strange eyes flashed wildly. Gazeem cowered in fright.

Slowly the rock began to grow. It expanded in all directions, changing shape. The eyes remained, and then ears formed, and a nose. Last came a mouth, huge and gaping. A column of white light burst from within, almost blinding Jafar.

The rock was now a tiger face, frozen in a furious, silent roar. Jafar stared in awe. His frightened parrot clung to his shoulder.

"Oh, no!" Gazeem murmured. "A Tiger-God!"

"At last, Iago!" Jafar said to his parrot. "After all my years of searching — the Cave of Wonders!"

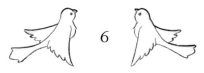

6

"*Awk!*" screeched Iago. "Cave of Wonders!"

Jafar pulled Gazeem close to him. "Bring me the lamp," he snarled. "The rest of the treasure is yours, but *the lamp is mine!*"

Gazeem swallowed hard. He began walking slowly towards the Tiger-God.

"*Awk!* The lamp!" Iago squawked, loud enough for Gazeem to hear. Then, leaning close to Jafar's ear, he whispered, "Jafar, where did you find this idiot?"

"Sssh!" Jafar snapped. Iago allowed no one to know that he could speak like a human – no one, that is, except his master. But right now, Jafar was in no mood to listen. He was too busy watching and waiting.

"*Who disturbs my slumber?*" boomed the Tiger-God, its voice shaking the ground again.

"Er… it is I, Gazeem, a humble thief," came the nervous, squeaky reply.

"*Know this!*" the Tiger-God said. "*Only one may enter here. One whose rags hide a heart that is pure – the Diamond in the Rough!*"

Gazeem cast a doubtful glance behind him. "Go on!" Jafar commanded.

Frightened, Gazeem turned back towards the cave. A flight of stairs led downwards into… what? He couldn't tell. Carefully, he began walking down.

RRRAAAUUUGGGHHH! The Tiger-God's thunderous roar was like nothing Jafar had ever heard. Gazeem's shriek could be heard for only a moment. Then the Tiger-God's mouth slammed shut, silencing the thief for ever.

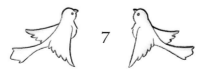

"*Seek thee out the Diamond in the Rough!*" the Tiger-God commanded.

Slowly, the rock collapsed into a mound of sand. The medallion halves flickered, then went dark.

Jafar stared in silence as Iago dived into the mound to retrieve the medallion halves. "I can't believe this!" the parrot said. "We're never going to get hold of that stupid lamp!"

"Patience, Iago," said Jafar. "Gazeem was obviously less than worthy."

"Now *there's* a big surprise!" said Iago, rolling his eyes. "So what are we going to do? We've got a big problem here…"

Jafar reached out and squeezed Iago's beak shut. He needed quiet. "Only one may enter…" he said. "I must find this one – this Diamond in the Rough."

The Diamond in the Rough – Jafar understood what that meant. A poor, common person who had shining qualities within.

There was only one way to find this person, and Jafar knew just how to do it.

An evil grin spread across his face. He hadn't got the treasure tonight, but no matter. He was close – oh, so close. And before long, his waiting would be over.

 8

"**S**top, thief!" shouted a guard at the top of his voice. He was chasing a ragged boy through the crowded marketplace of Agrabah.

The boy, Aladdin, zigzagged skilfully round the stalls – fruit sellers, clothing merchants, bakers, trinket sellers. In his right hand, he clutched a loaf of bread. Beside him ran a small monkey dressed in a waistcoat and hat.

"I'll get you, street rat!" the guard shouted.

Street rat. If there was one name Aladdin hated, that was it. The Sultan's guards looked down on the poor people of Agrabah – people such as himself. Yes, he did sometimes steal food. He had no choice – he had to eat. But he was no street rat.

"Come on, Abu!" Aladdin called to his pet monkey. He ran to a nearby house and leapt onto its low, flat roof. Then he and Abu sprinted from rooftop to rooftop, landing on a pair of clotheslines and finally falling into a soft pile of washing.

Instantly Aladdin was snatched up by a pair of thick, hairy hands.

It was Rasoul, the head of the Sultan's guard. Rasoul was a man of few words, but if there was one thing he did well, it was catching young thieves.

"Gotcha!" Rasoul said, lifting Aladdin up.

Abu leapt onto Rasoul's shoulder and shoved the guard's turban over his eyes. Aladdin quickly wrenched himself free, and he and Abu bolted away. They wove through the marketplace, past a camel salesman, a rug merchant, a jewellery cart...

Suddenly Abu stopped. The little monkey's eyes were fixed on the cart.

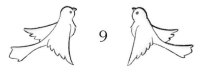

Abu had one big weakness—sparkling jewels. He crouched beside the cart, reaching up to steal a pendant.

"Stop him!" someone yelled. Dozens of faces turned towards Abu.

Aladdin spun round. He grabbed Abu by the scruff of the neck and dragged him towards a tall tower. Leaving the angry crowd behind, they raced up a staircase and leapt through an open window at the other side of the building. They landed safely in a quiet, dark alley, and sat down.

They were *starving*.

"All right, Abu, now we feast!" he said, breaking the bread in half.

As he opened his mouth to take a bite, Aladdin saw a frail boy and girl in the shadows. They said nothing, but their wide, staring eyes spoke for them. Aladdin could tell they hadn't eaten for days.

He looked at the bread. He had risked his life to get it—and now his mouth was watering. But he couldn't let these children go hungry. With a sigh, he held out his meal to them. "Go on, take it," he said softly.

Abu scowled, but slowly handed over his piece of bread, too. The little girl smiled at him.

As chilly darkness settled over Agrabah that night, Aladdin and Abu climbed to the roof of a crumbling, old building. There were only a few mats and some worn-out pillows, but to Aladdin and Abu, this was home.

Aladdin gazed out across the starlit town towards the Sultan's palace, which loomed majestically in the distance. "Some day, Abu, things are going to be different. We'll be dressed in robes instead of rags. We'll be rich, live in a palace and never have any problems. That would be the life, eh, Abu?"

But Abu had curled up on a pillow and was now fast asleep.

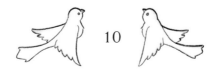

CHAPTER THREE

"*Y*EEEOOOW!*"

The scream from the palace menagerie echoed into the throne room. A moment later – *WHACK!* The door slammed against the throne room wall. In stormed an angry prince. His name was Achmed. "I've never been so insulted!" he shouted. "Good luck finding a husband for *her!*"

"But... but..." the Sultan spluttered.

The Prince marched right past him and out through the other door, revealing a large hole in the seat of his trousers.

"Jasmine!" the Sultan bellowed. He was a roly-poly old man, happy and kind, and loved by his subjects. Only one person could upset him – his daughter, Princess Jasmine. He loved her dearly, but she was so... stubborn. All he wanted her to do was to marry a prince. Every princess did it. But Jasmine? *No.* No one was good enough for her!

He waddled into the palace menagerie. The sound of water was all around, flowing from marble waterways, spouting into pools from hand-carved fountains. It was the most beautiful place in all Agrabah. But the Sultan noticed none of that now. "Jasmine!" he called again.

"*RRRRRRR,*" came a soft growl.

There was a flash of orange and black. Suddenly the Sultan found himself face to face with a tiger, who held the missing piece of Prince Achmed's trousers in his teeth.

"Confound it, Rajah!" the Sultan said, grabbing the torn material.

Rajah slunk away to the back of the garden, where the Princess sat at the edge of a fountain. "Oh, Father, Rajah was only playing," she said, gently stroking the tiger. "You were just playing with that overdressed, self-absorbed Prince Achmed, weren't you?" she said to Rajah.

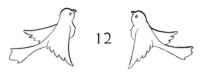

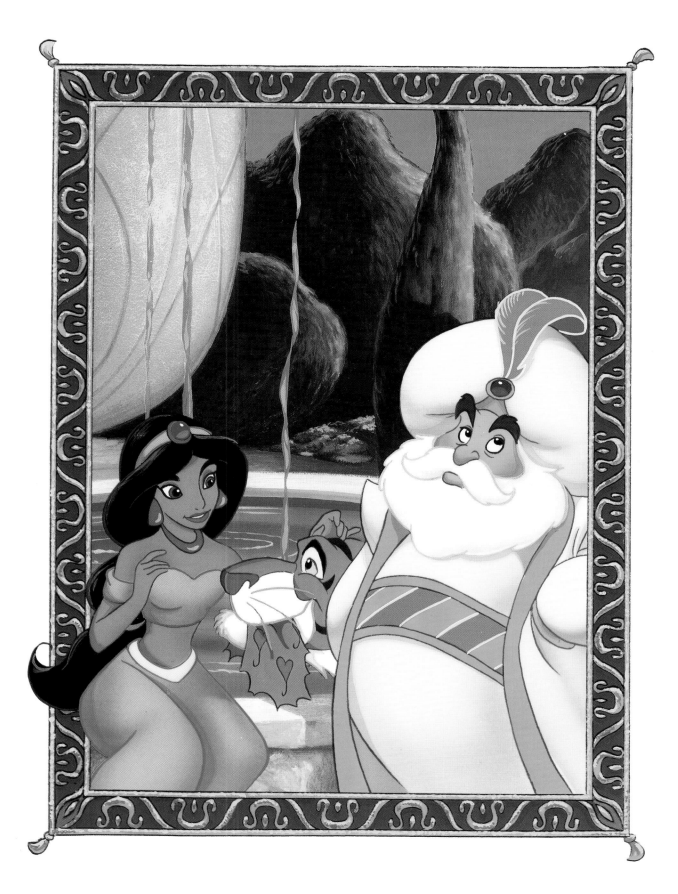

Jasmine was more than beautiful. Princes from lands afar risked their lives crossing the desert to see her. Each vowed to conquer the world for her love.

But as for Jasmine — well, she'd had enough of half-witted princes and bragging noblemen. If only one of them would show a little intelligence. Some kindness, honesty and a sense of humour wouldn't go amiss, either.

The Sultan shook his head. "Dearest, you've got to stop rejecting every suitor. The law says you must be married to a prince by your next birthday. You have only three more days."

"The law is *wrong!*" Jasmine replied. "Father, I hate being forced to marry. If I do marry, I want it to be for love."

"It's not just the law," the Sultan said gently. He hesitated for a minute before continuing. "I'm not going to be around for ever, and I want to make sure you're taken care of."

"But I've never done anything on my own! I've never had any real friends — except you, Rajah," Jasmine said, giving her tiger a pat on the head. "I've never even been outside the palace walls!"

"But Jasmine, you're a princess!" cried the Sultan.

"Then maybe I don't *want* to be a princess any longer!"

"Ooooooohh!" The Sultan threw up his hands in exasperation and shuffled back into the throne room.

A shadow appeared behind him. It was the tall, thin shadow of a man in a pointed turban, with a parrot on his shoulder. In his right hand was a long staff with a snake's head carved at the top.

The Sultan turned round. "Ah, Jafar, my most trusted adviser!" he said. "I am in desperate need of your wisdom."

"My life is but to serve you," said Jafar with a tight, thin-lipped smile.

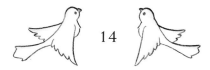

"Jasmine refuses to choose a husband," the Sultan said. "I am at my wits' end!"

"*Awk!* Wits' end!" Iago squawked.

The Sultan took some biscuits out of a china bowl. "Here you are, Pretty Polly," he said, offering them to the parrot.

If there was one thing Iago hated, it was biscuits. Especially the dry, stale biscuits the Sultan always gave him. He nearly choked as the Sultan crammed the biscuits into his beak.

"Your Majesty certainly has a way with dumb animals," Jafar remarked. "Now then, I may be able to find a solution to your problem, but it would require the use of your Blue Diamond."

The Sultan backed away, clutching at the ring on his finger.

"My ring has been in the family for years..." he protested.

Jafar held his staff in front of the Sultan's eyes. The eyes of the snake's head began to glow. "It's necessary to find the Princess a suitor, isn't it?" Jafar said, moving closer. "Don't worry... everything will be fine."

The Sultan could not stop staring at the snake's head. His willpower was draining away. "Everything will be fine," he droned as he slipped the ring off his finger and gave it to Jafar.

Jafar smiled. "You are most gracious, Sire," he said. "Now run along and play with your toys, hmmm?"

"Yes," the Sultan said dreamily, waddling away.

Jafar turned and left the throne room. As he hurried down a marble corridor, Iago began spitting out the biscuits. "I can't take it any more! If I have to choke down one more of those mouldy, disgusting biscuits, I'll grab him by the neck and..."

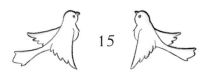

"Calm yourself, Iago," said Jafar. "This Blue Diamond will reveal to us the Diamond in the Rough—the one who can enter the cave and bring us the lamp."

At the end of the corridor, Jafar entered his private quarters. "Soon *I* will be Sultan, not that jumbo portion of stupidity!"

"And then," Iago crowed, "I'll shove biscuits down *his* throat!"

At the other end of the dark room, Jafar pushed open a hidden door, revealing a spiral staircase. He began climbing the stairs that led to his secret laboratory. In every corner of the room, potions bubbled in glass beakers. There was a huge cauldron at the back and an enormous hourglass on an old table.

Jafar walked towards the hourglass, holding the Blue Diamond. "Now, Iago, we go to work."

∽∘∽

Early the next morning, Jasmine crept to the palace wall in disguise. A dejected Rajah followed close behind, his head hanging in sadness.

"I'm sorry, Rajah," Jasmine said, "but I can't stay here and have my life lived for me."

Tears welled up inside her. It was hard enough running away from her father. But having to look into Rajah's eyes made it more painful than she could have imagined.

She had to make her move now, otherwise she might change her mind. Stepping onto Rajah's back, Jasmine quickly climbed the garden wall. Pausing at the top, she said, "I'll miss you, Rajah. Goodbye."

Then she disappeared over the side, into the land of her subjects—a land she had never visited before.

CHAPTER FOUR

"**B**reakfast is served, Abu!" said Aladdin as he cracked open a ripe, juicy melon. Perched on an awning, the two friends had a perfect view of the bustling marketplace below. All round them, merchants hawked their wares. "Buy a pot – brass and silver!" called one.

"Sugared dates and figs!" shouted another as he strolled by a crowd of people watching a fire breather. "Pistachio nuts! Let the fire breather roast them for you!"

"Fresh fish!" cried a third vendor. Aladdin watched as the man waved a large fish high in the air, almost smacking it into the face of a young girl who was covered with a thin cloak. She staggered backwards, bumping right into the fire breather. He belched out a long plume of fire.

"Oh!" cried the startled girl. "Excuse me. I'm sorry!"

Aladdin stopped eating. He couldn't help staring. Maybe it was her eyes, so deep and kind. Or her hair, like a cascade of the blackest silk. Or her perfect skin, or her…

Aladdin blushed. He *never* thought of girls that way. But this one – well, this one was different. Special somehow.

∽○∽

Jasmine spotted a ragged little boy standing in a daze in front of a mound of ripe fruit. "You must be hungry," she said, taking an apple from the cart. "Here you are."

The child beamed. Clutching the apple, he ran away.

"You'd better pay for that!" the vendor said.

"Pay?" Jasmine looked puzzled. She had never paid for anything in her life.

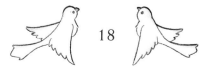

"I'm sorry, sir, I don't have any money. But I'm sure I can get some from the Sultan."

"Thief!" shouted the fruit seller, grabbing her arm. With his other hand, he pulled out a shiny knife. "Do you know what the penalty is for stealing?"

Suddenly Aladdin darted between them and grabbed the fruit seller's arm. "Thank you, kind sir, I'm so glad you found my sister!" he said. Turning to Jasmine, he scolded, "I've been looking all over for you!" Jasmine was about to protest when Aladdin whispered, "Just play along."

The fruit seller pulled Aladdin aside. "You know this girl?" he asked. "She said she knew the Sultan!"

"She's my sister," Aladdin replied. Then, lowering his voice, he said, "Sadly, she's a little crazy. She thinks the monkey is the Sultan."

Quickly Jasmine began bowing to Abu. "O Wise Sultan," she said, "how may I serve you?"

People in the crowd began to laugh. "Now come along, Sis," Aladdin said, helping her up. "Time to see the doctor."

As the fruit seller stared at Aladdin and Jasmine, Abu snatched some apples off the cart and stuffed them into his waistcoat.

Jasmine stopped in front of a camel and said, "Hello, Doctor, how are you?"

"No, no, not that one," Aladdin said. "Come on, Sis." Looking over his shoulder, he called, "Come on, Sultan!"

Abu scurried after them, puffing out his chest in imitation of the Sultan. Suddenly three apples tumbled out of his waistcoat.

The fruit seller turned red with fury. "Come back here, you little thieves!" he shrieked.

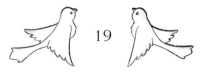

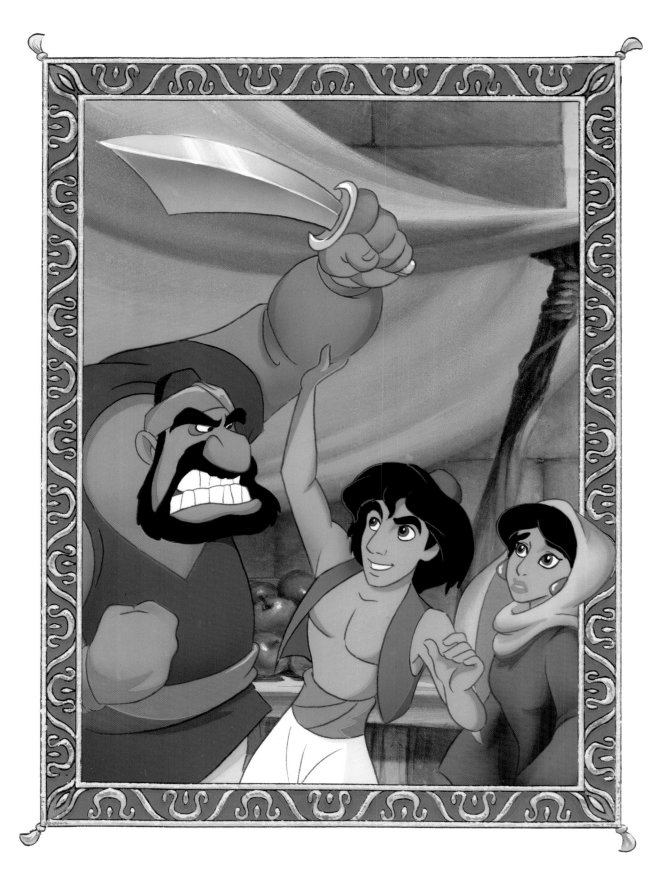

But it was too late. The three of them broke into a run and disappeared into the crowd.

⌒○⌒

At the palace, Jafar chuckled with evil glee. Iago was frantically turning a wheel that was attached to a generator. Electricity spurted from the generator into a bubbling cauldron. Slowly a shimmering blue cloud formed in the air.

The Blue Diamond was encased in a frame above an enormous hourglass. Jafar swept his arm in front of it, chanting, "Part, sands of time! Reveal to me the one who can enter the cave!"

He flipped the hourglass over. Then, with a loud *CRRRACK!* a bolt of lightning shot from the cloud. It struck the diamond, which exploded into a pulsing blue light.

The sand in the hourglass began to glow and swirl. Slowly an image began to form – an image of Aladdin running through the marketplace.

"That's the clown we've been waiting for?" Iago blurted out.

"Yes, a ragged little urchin. How perfect – he'll never be missed!" Jafar looked at Iago with a twisted grin. "Let's get the guards to invite him to the palace, shall we?"

⌒○⌒

Aladdin, Abu and Jasmine jumped from rooftop to rooftop in the marketplace. Aladdin could tell that Jasmine had never been to that part of Agrabah before. But he had to admit that when it came to roof hopping, she learned quickly.

When Aladdin and Abu finally reached their home, Jasmine looked around and said, "Is this where you live?"

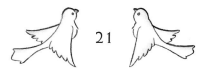

21

"Yep, just me and Abu," Aladdin replied. "It's not much, but it has a great view." He pointed towards the palace. "Amazing, huh? I wonder what it would be like to live there and have servants and valets…"

Jasmine sighed. "And people who tell you where to go and how to dress."

"That's better than here," Aladdin replied. "Always scraping for food and ducking guards…"

"Never being free to make your own choices," Jasmine said. "Always feeling…"

"*Trapped*," they said at the same time. Their eyes met, and they smiled. Aladdin blushed, then quickly took an apple from Abu and tossed it to Jasmine. "So where are you from?" he asked, changing the subject.

"What does it matter?" Jasmine replied. "I ran away, and I'm not going back. My father wanted to force me to get married."

"That's awful!" Aladdin said.

Jasmine's eyes met his again. Suddenly Aladdin couldn't speak, couldn't even move. Strange feelings raced round inside him, feelings so strong they made him dizzy. Who *was* this mysterious girl?

∾ ○ ∾

"*Here* you are!" roared a deep voice behind them.

Aladdin snapped out of his trance. On the steps stood a group of the Sultan's guards, swords drawn.

"*They're after me!*" Aladdin and Jasmine said together. They stopped, looked at each other in confusion, then spoke again at the same time, "They're after *you?*"

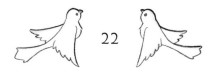

But there was no time to figure things out. Aladdin looked over the opposite side of the roof. There was a pile of hay below. "Do you trust me?" he asked Jasmine, pulling her close. Their eyes locked again.

"Well... yes," she replied.

"Then *jump*!"

Aladdin, Jasmine and Abu leapt off the roof. They landed safely in the hay and quickly got to their feet. Aladdin spun round, ready to sprint for his life.

But it was too late. Rasoul loomed over him, smirking. "We just keep running into each other, eh, street rat? It's the dungeon for you, boy!"

Jasmine stepped into Rasoul's path. "Let him go!" she ordered.

"Look, a street *mouse*!" Rasoul snarled. With a laugh, he pushed Jasmine to the ground.

Jasmine sprang to her feet. Anger flashed in her eyes. Regally drawing back her hood, she said in a firm, commanding voice, "Unhand him, by order of the Princess!"

"The *Princess*?" Aladdin repeated.

The guards froze in shock. "Princess Jasmine?" Rasoul said. "What – what are you doing outside the palace?"

"Just do as I command," said Jasmine. "Release him."

"I would, Princess," Rasoul replied, "but my orders come from Jafar. You'll have to take it up with him."

And with a sheepish shrug, he dragged Aladdin away.

"Believe me, I will!" Jasmine exclaimed.

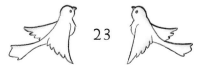

23

Back at the palace, Jasmine stormed into Jafar's chamber. She found him looking as devious and sinister as ever. "Princess," he said, "how may I be of service?"

Princess Jasmine looked him sharply in the eye. "Jafar, the guards just took a boy from the market—on your orders."

"Your father has charged me with keeping peace in Agrabah," Jafar said. "The boy was a criminal. He tried to kidnap you."

"He didn't *kidnap* me!" Jasmine replied. "I ran away!"

Jafar's brow creased with concern. "Oh dear, how frightfully upsetting. Had I but known..." His voice trailed off.

"What do you mean?" Jasmine asked.

"Sadly, the boy's sentence has already been carried out."

Jasmine shuddered. "What sentence?"

Jafar sighed and put his hand on Jasmine's shoulder. "Death," he said softly, "by beheading."

"How—how *could* you?" Jasmine gasped.

Then she turned and ran out, not stopping until she reached the menagerie.

Rajah bounded happily towards her, but Jasmine ran right past him. She collapsed by a fountain, tears running down her cheeks.

Do you trust me? the boy had asked her. Yes, she had. This boy was so different from the others—funny, kind, friendly...

And now he was dead. Because of a stupid mistake.

"Oh, Rajah," she said, "this is all my fault. I didn't even know his name."

Jasmine buried her head in Rajah's fur and wept.

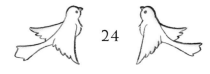

CHAPTER FIVE

The palace dungeon was cold, dark and dirty. Not even the Sultan had ever entered it. All prisoners were brought there by Jafar – and not one had escaped.

Aladdin was determined to be the first. He grunted loudly, struggling against his chains, but they held fast to the stone wall.

Jafar had lied to Jasmine. Aladdin was alive – but he wouldn't be for long, if everything went according to Jafar's plan.

Aladdin collapsed to the floor with a sigh. "She was the *Princess*," he said to himself. "I can't believe it!"

Just then a shadow appeared on the wall – the shadow of a small monkey poised between the bars of the prison window. "Abu!" Aladdin cried. "Down here!"

Abu hopped down. He frowned at Aladdin and chattered angrily as he did an imitation of a pretty girl walking.

Aladdin knew he was being scolded for paying too much attention to Jasmine. "But she was in trouble," he said. "Anyway, I'll never see her again. I'm a street rat, remember? Besides, there's some law that says she's got to marry a prince." He sighed with frustration. "She deserves a prince."

Abu pulled a small pick out of his waistcoat pocket and unlocked Aladdin's handcuffs. Grinning with triumph, he pulled Aladdin towards the window.

But Aladdin just slumped to the floor. He was still thinking of Jasmine. "I'm a fool," he said.

"You're only a fool if you give up," came a crackly voice.

Aladdin turned to see a broken-toothed old man hobble out of the shadows. His white beard hung down to his knees, and he had a hump on his back. He looked as if he had been in the dungeon for years. "Who are you?" Aladdin asked.

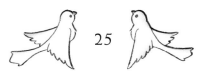

"I am a lowly prisoner like yourself—but together, perhaps we can be more. I know of a cave filled with treasures beyond your wildest dreams." The man shuffled closer, smiling. "There's treasure enough to impress your princess, I'd wager."

At the mention of treasure, Abu's eyes lit up. He tugged at Aladdin's waistcoat. Neither of them saw Iago peep out of the old man's tattered shirt and whisper, "Jafar, would you hurry up? I'm dying in here!"

Aladdin gave the prisoner a forlorn look. "But the law says she has to marry…"

Jafar raised a bony finger and spoke once again in an old man's voice. "Haven't you heard of the Golden Rule? Whoever has the gold makes the rules!"

"Why would you share this treasure with me?" said Aladdin.

"I need a young pair of legs and a strong back to go in after it." Jafar pushed one of the stones in the wall. Slowly an entire section of the dungeon wall opened, revealing a hidden stairway. "So, do we have a deal?" he asked Aladdin.

Aladdin hesitated, but finally shook the old man's hand.

Jafar cackled with excitement. "We're off!"

ကာ ∘ ကာ

It was dark by the time they reached the Cave of Wonders. Jafar took out the medallion pieces and fitted them together once again.

Aladdin stared in awe as the pieces flew into the sandstone and the massive Tiger-God arose.

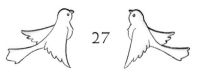

"Who disturbs my slumber?" the terrifying voice boomed. Jafar motioned Aladdin to go closer.

Abu jumped into Aladdin's waistcoat. Aladdin tried to stop himself trembling. "Uh, it is I... Aladdin."

A tunnel of harsh light shot from the Tiger-God's mouth. *"Proceed,"* the voice continued. *"Touch nothing but the lamp."*

"Quickly, my boy," Jafar urged in his old man's voice. "Fetch the lamp, and then you shall have your reward!"

Cautiously Aladdin stepped inside the Tiger-God's mouth. Through the blinding light, he saw a long stairway leading down. At the bottom there were piles of gold. Mountains of gold. Coins, jewels, plates, bowls, goblets, chests, all heaped together as far as he could see.

Abu, almost hypnotized by the sight of all that gold, went straight for an enormous treasure chest.

"Abu!" Aladdin warned. "Don't touch *anything*! We have to find that lamp."

Abu grumbled, but turned from the chest and followed his master through the cave—until he sensed a strange movement behind him. He spun round to look.

Nothing—just a purple carpet with gold tassels, lying on the floor. Abu turned and ran towards Aladdin.

This time something tapped Abu on the shoulder, then snatched his hat. Abu spun round again.

It was the carpet, walking along behind him.

"EEEEEEEEEE!" Abu shrieked, jumping onto Aladdin for protection. The frightened carpet quickly hid behind a large pile of coins.

"Stop it, Abu!" Aladdin said.

Abu jabbered away, pointing to the mound of coins. Aladdin turned and saw a tassel peep out, then quickly pull itself back.

Aladdin moved closer for a better look. He could see the carpet moving away from him. "A magic carpet!" he said. Then he called, "Come on out! We're not going to hurt you."

Using its two lower tassels as legs and its upper ones as hands, the carpet slowly emerged and handed Aladdin Abu's hat. Aladdin's mouth hung open in disbelief.

Abu snatched the hat and began scolding the carpet. The carpet slowly walked away, drooped over in shame. "Hey, wait a minute, don't go!" Aladdin said. "Maybe you can help us to find this lamp?"

The carpet whirled round and pointed excitedly. Aladdin grinned. "I think he knows where it is!"

Rising off the ground, the carpet began to fly. Aladdin and Abu followed it into another cavern.

Suddenly Aladdin stopped in his tracks. This cavern made the other one look like a waiting room. It stretched upwards so high that Aladdin couldn't see the ceiling. The walls were a cool blue, unlike any colour he had ever seen in the city. A lagoon of blue water stretched from wall to wall.

In the centre of the lake stood a tower of solid rock with only a series of stepping stones leading to it. On top, lit by a magical beam of light, was a small object.

It was too far away to see, but Aladdin knew that it had to be the lamp. His heart began to race. It wouldn't be easy to get to the top. First he would have to skip across the rocks, then he would have to climb the steep tower.

"Wait here," he said to Abu and the carpet. "And remember, don't touch *anything*."

Springing from stone to stone, Aladdin arrived at the base of the tower. With a sudden groan, the sloping rock changed into a staircase.

Aladdin smiled. Someone—*something*—was on his side. He raced up, two steps at a time.

At the top, the lamp came clearly into view.

It was dusty, dented and cheaper-looking than the oldest used lamp he had ever seen in the marketplace.

Aladdin picked it up. "This is it?" he said to himself. "This is what we came all the way here for?"

Out of the corner of his eye, he spotted Abu and the carpet. They were in front of a large golden statue that looked like a giant monkey idol. Its arms were outstretched, and in its cupped palms it held an enormous red jewel.

And Abu was reaching straight for it.

"Abu!" Aladdin shouted. *"No!"*

But it was too late. Abu had the jewel in his hands.

Instantly, the ground began to rumble. Rocks and dust fell from above. The voice of the Tiger-God echoed like a cannon. *"Infidels! You have touched the forbidden treasures! Now you will never again see the light of day!"*

The jewel began to melt in Abu's grip. Panicking, he put it back into the statue's hands.

But the damage had already been done. The stairway beneath Aladdin was transformed into a long chute, and his feet gave way.

With a last-minute lunge, Aladdin grabbed the lamp. As he tumbled down the chute, he saw the lagoon become a pool of boiling lava. He closed his eyes, bracing himself for the end.

WHOOSH! He stopped in midair. Something was pushing him upwards. His eyes sprang open.

The carpet had caught him, and it was whisking him away.

The cavern shook violently. Aladdin held tightly onto the carpet. It dodged right and left as large rocks fell from the ceiling. Aladdin looked down, searching for Abu.

"EEEEEE!" came a cry from below. There was Abu, hopping across the stepping stones and screeching. Over his head, a boulder hurtled towards him.

With a burst of speed, the carpet streaked down. Aladdin plucked Abu out of danger, and the carpet flew towards the cavern entrance. The ground below erupted as the piles of dazzling treasures burst into flames. Aladdin and Abu looked down in horror. The coins and jewels were melting!

The carpet, charred by a wave of lava, raced to the stairway. They could see the starry night sky through the entrance above. There was not far to go now.

THUNK! A jagged piece of rock fell onto the carpet, pinning it to the ground.

Aladdin and Abu tumbled onto the stairs.

Aladdin looked down at the carpet in dismay. There was no way he could save it. It would be hard enough to save himself.

He looked up. He could see the opening at the top – and freedom. Abu scaled the steps and hopped outside.

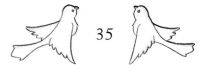

Aladdin followed as fast as he could, but the stairs began to shake and he lost his footing.

Springing to his feet, he lunged for the top step. His fingers grabbed at it—just as the entire stairway buckled beneath him.

Aladdin dangled over the collapsing cave. "Help me!" he cried. "I can't hold on!"

Still dressed as the beggar, Jafar peeped over the edge. "First give me the lamp!"

There was no time to argue. Aladdin held it out.

Jafar's eyes gleamed as he grabbed the lamp and thrust it into his robe. "At last!" he shrieked in triumph. Then, leering at Aladdin, he pulled out a dagger.

"What are you doing?" cried Aladdin.

"Giving you your reward," Jafar replied. "Your *eternal* reward!"

Abu leapt at Jafar, biting him hard on the arm.

"*YEEEAAGGGH!*" Jafar screamed. He fought desperately, but Abu held on tight.

Finally Jafar dropped the dagger. Enraged, he flung Abu into the cave.

Aladdin's fingers could hold on no longer. He let go.

The walls raced by him as he and Abu tumbled, head over heels, into the cavern below.

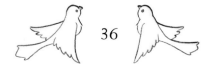

CHAPTER SIX

Aladdin awoke on the cave floor. On top of him lay the carpet and Abu. The fire was out, the lava gone; only the steady drip of water echoed throughout the cave.

Aladdin groaned and sat up. The carpet fell off, and Abu began to stir. Above him, Aladdin could see no opening, only the solid ceiling of the cavern.

"We're trapped!" he said. "That two-faced son of a jackal! By now he's long gone with that lamp."

Abu jumped up. Something bulged in his waistcoat – Aladdin thought it must be a jewel. Like a magician, Abu waved his arms, reached into his waistcoat, and pulled out the hidden object.

Aladdin blinked and shook his head in disbelief. It was the lamp!

"Why, you little thief!" Aladdin said with a smile. He took the battered lamp and studied it closely. "There's something written on it, but it's hard to make out."

In an effort to get the grime off, Aladdin began rubbing the faded words with the edge of his waistcoat. He rubbed harder and harder – then suddenly stopped.

The lamp was glowing!

Aladdin gasped. Abu and the carpet backed away.

Suddenly – *POOOOF!* Colourful smoke erupted from the lamp's spout. It whirled crazily, growing into a blue cloud, then slowly taking on a shape – an enormous flowing shape with arms, a chest, a head and a wild-eyed face with a long, curling black beard.

"Ten thousand years will give you *such* a crick in the neck!" the blue creature said.

"I must have hit my head harder than I thought," said Aladdin, wide-eyed. He pinched himself to make sure he wasn't dreaming.

Meanwhile, the creature was holding his own head and twisting it round. "Wow, does that feel good!" he said. "And it's nice to be back. Hi! What's your name?" he asked Aladdin.

"Uh… Aladdin!"

"Hello, Aladdin! Can I call you Al? Or maybe just Din? You know, you're a lot smaller than my last master!"

"I'm your *master?*" asked Aladdin, dumbfounded.

"That's right! And I am your Genie, direct from the lamp, here for your wish fulfilment! You get three wishes, to be exact."

"Three wishes?" said Aladdin. "Any three I want?"

"Well, almost," replied the Genie. "There are a few limitations…

Rule number one – I can't kill anybody, so don't ask.

Rule number two – I can't make anybody fall in love with anybody else.

Rule number three – I can't bring anybody back from the dead. Other than that, you've got it!"

"Limitations," Aladdin sighed. "Some all-powerful Genie. You probably can't even get us out of this cave."

The Genie put his hands on his hips. "Excuse me?" he said. "You don't believe me?" Jumping onto the carpet, he scooped up Aladdin and Abu in his mammoth hands. "You're getting your wishes, so sit down and we're out of here!"

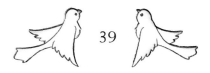

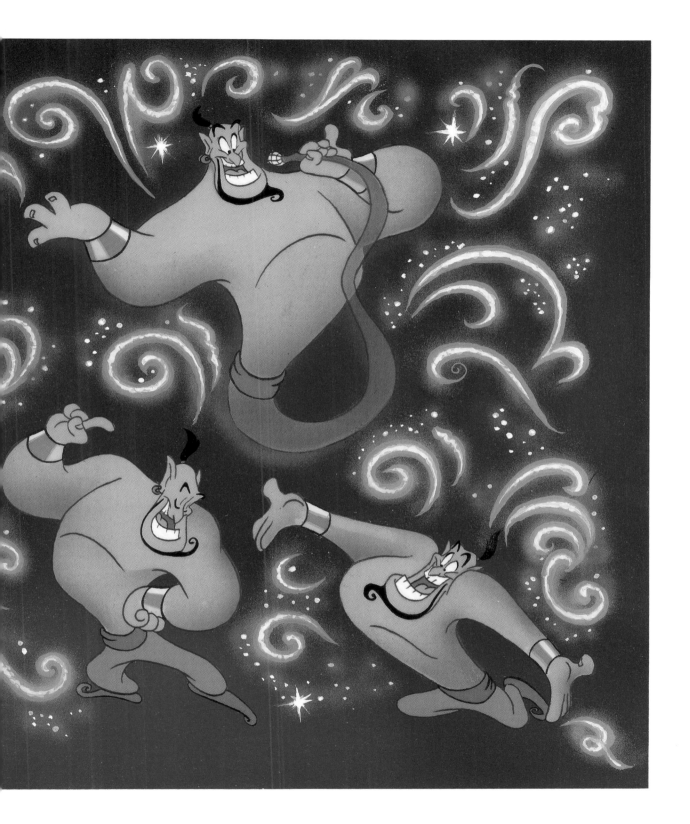

CHAPTER SEVEN

"**Z**afar, this is an outrage!" the Sultan yelled, pacing the throne room. "From now on, you're to discuss sentencing of prisoners with me — *before* they are beheaded!"

Princess Jasmine scowled at Jafar as he bowed his head. "My humblest apologies to both of you," said Jafar.

"At least *some* good will come of my being forced to marry," Jasmine said. "When I am Queen, I will have the power to get rid of *you*, Jafar!" With that, she stalked out to the menagerie.

"Jasmine!" the Sultan called, running after her.

Jafar watched them leave. His sad, sorrowful look began to disappear, and all his rage and frustration bubbled up. "If only I had got that lamp," he muttered through clenched teeth.

"To think we've got to keep sweet-talking that chump and his chump daughter for the rest of our lives," said Iago.

"Until she finds a chump *husband*," Jafar remarked. "Then she'll have us banished — or beheaded!"

"Wait a minute, Jafar!" Iago said. "What if *you* marry the Princess? Then you become the Sultan, right?"

Jafar walked slowly to the throne and sat down. It felt *wonderful!* "Hmmm," he said. "The idea has merit!"

"Yeah!" Iago squawked. "And then we drop Papa-in-law and the little woman off a cliff — *KER-SPLAT!*"

Jafar burst out laughing. "I love the way your foul little mind works!"

∽○∽

A thunderous boom resounded above the cave, its ceiling opened and early-morning light poured in. The carpet spiralled upwards, picking up speed.

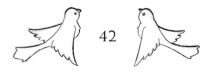

Aladdin held on tight and laughed with joy. He was free!

And he still had three wishes left.

The carpet swooped down to the sand on a desert oasis just outside Agrabah. The Genie turned to Aladdin with a proud grin. "Well, how about that, huh? Do you doubt me now?"

"No," said Aladdin. "Now, about my three wishes…"

"*Three?*" the Genie said. "You are down by one, boy!"

Aladdin smiled mischievously. "I never actually *wished* to get out of the cave. You did that on your own!"

The Genie thought for a moment. "All right," he said with a laugh. "You win. But no more freebies!"

Aladdin hopped off the carpet and began pacing up and down. "Hmm… three wishes… What would *you* wish for?"

"Me? No one's ever asked me that before." The Genie thought it over for a moment. "Well, in my case – freedom."

"You mean you're a prisoner?" Aladdin asked.

"That's what being a Genie's all about," the Genie said with a shrug. "Phenomenal cosmic powers, itty-bitty living space."

The carpet, Abu and Aladdin peered inside the small lamp. "Genie, that's terrible," Aladdin said.

"To be free, to be my own master – that would be greater than all the magic and treasures in the world," the Genie sighed. "But the only way I can get out is for my master to wish me out, and you can guess how often that's happened."

Aladdin thought about this for a moment. "I'll do it," he finally said. "I'll set you free."

"Yeah, right," the Genie said, rolling his eyes.

"No, I'm not lying," Aladdin said. "I promise – after my first two wishes, I'll use my third wish to set you free."

"Okay, here's hoping!" said the Genie. "Now, what is it *you* want?"

"Well," said Aladdin, "there's this girl…"

"Wrong!" interrupted the Genie. "I can't make anyone fall in love, remember?"

"But, Genie, she's clever and fun and beautiful…" Aladdin shrugged and looked at the ground. "But she's the Princess. Even to have a chance, I'd have to be – *hey!*" Aladdin's eyes suddenly lit up. "Can you make me… a prince?"

The Genie raised an eyebrow. "Is that an official wish? Say the magic words!"

"Genie, I wish to become a prince!" Aladdin blurted.

"*All right!*" The Genie began circling round Aladdin. "Now, first we have to get rid of the fez-and-waistcoat combo." With a sweeping gesture, he conjured up a flowing cloak of fine silk, a gold-trimmed shirt and trousers, and a turban with a dazzling jewel and a magnificent plume.

"*Wow!*" Aladdin breathed. He could hardly believe how… *princely* he looked. No one would dare to call him *street rat* now. He picked up the lamp and hid it under his turban. After all, no decent prince would be seen with such a piece of junk.

"Hmmm, you'll need some transport," the Genie was saying. He looked at Abu. "Excuse me! Monkey boy!"

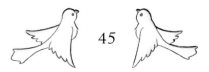

Abu shot away, trying to hide. But it was no use. With a snap of his fingers, the Genie turned him into a camel.

"Not good enough," the Genie said, snapping his fingers again. This time Abu became a handsome stallion. "Still not enough…"

With a decisive snap, Abu was transformed again, this time into an elephant. "That's it!" the Genie said at last. "What better way to make your entrance down the streets of Agrabah than riding your very own elephant!"

Aladdin could only stare in amazement. But the Genie was more excited than ever. He gestured wildly, laughing at the top of his voice. "Hang on to your turban, kid!" he shouted. "We're going to make you a star!"

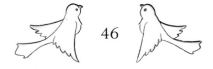

CHAPTER EIGHT

Jafar rushed into the throne room, holding a large scroll. "Sire," he called to the Sultan, "I have found a solution to the problem with your daughter!"

"*Awk!*" squawked Iago. "Problem with your daughter!"

"It's right here," said Jafar as he unfurled the scroll and began to read, "*If a princess has not chosen a husband by her sixteenth birthday, then the Sultan shall choose for her!*"

"But Jasmine hated all those suitors," said the Sultan. "How can I choose someone she might hate?"

"Not to worry, there is more," said Jafar, unrolling the scroll further. "*In the event a suitable prince cannot be found, a princess may be wed to...* hmmm, interesting..."

"What?" the Sultan demanded. "Who?"

"*The Royal Vizier.*" Jafar looked up. "Why, that's *me!*"

"But I thought the law says only a prince can marry a princess," the Sultan said, reaching for the scroll.

Jafar quickly set it on a table and picked up his staff. "Desperate times call for desperate measures, my lord."

The snake's head began to glow with hypnotic light. "Yes," said the Sultan, his eyes glazing over. "Desperate times..."

"You will order the Princess to marry me," Jafar said confidently.

"I will order the Princess to..."

RA-TA-TA-TAAAAAAAH! The sound of trumpets blared in through the window. The Sultan blinked and turned towards the noise. "Wha—what? I heard something!"

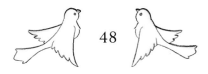

Instantly the spell was broken. The Sultan rushed to the window and looked out. Jafar followed, muttering.

A huge band was marching down the main street. A giant peacock float moved slowly behind; lions and bears in colourful, painted cages rolled by. People filled the streets to watch the grand spectacle.

"Make way for Prince Ali Ababwa!" the bandleader sang. Behind him strode a majestic elephant, its trunk held proudly in the air. On its back, a canopy bounced up and down. And just in front of the canopy was Aladdin, grinning and waving.

The crowd roared in admiration. Dancers whirled, swordsmen marched in perfect step and dozens of attendants walked alongside the procession. Abu the elephant lumbered on proudly, and the carpet made a perfect cushion on Abu's bumpy back.

The Genie floated among the crowd, changing himself every few minutes into a drum major, a harem dancer, an old man, a child. In each disguise, he told everyone what a splendid prince was approaching.

By the time Aladdin reached the palace gates, he was the talk of Agrabah. His entire entourage – Abu, swordsmen, brass band, dancers, and all – marched right into the throne room.

As the Sultan and Jafar stared, Aladdin slid off Abu's back. "Your Majesty," he said, bowing before the Sultan, "I have journeyed from afar to seek your daughter's hand."

"Prince Ali Ababwa!" the Sultan said with a bright smile. "I'm delighted to meet you. This is my Royal Vizier, Jafar."

Jafar did not look delighted at all. "I'm afraid, Prince Abooboo…"

"Ababwa," Aladdin corrected him.

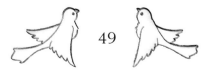

"Whatever," Jafar said. "You cannot just parade in here uninvited and..."

"What a remarkable device!" the Sultan suddenly exclaimed, looking at the carpet. "May I try?"

"Why, certainly, Your Majesty!" Aladdin said. He helped the Sultan onto the carpet. It took off, flying the Sultan around the room.

As the old man hooted with delight, Jafar eyed Aladdin suspiciously. "Just where did you say you were from?" he asked.

Before Aladdin could answer, the carpet swooped down and let the Sultan off. "Well, this is a very impressive prince, indeed!" Lowering his voice, the Sultan said to Jafar, "If we're lucky, you won't have to marry Jasmine after all! Yes, Jasmine will like this one."

"And I'm sure I'll like Princess Jasmine," Aladdin said.

"Your Highness!" Jafar blurted. "On Jasmine's behalf, I must say..."

"Just let her meet me," Aladdin interrupted. "*I* will win your daughter."

None of them had seen Jasmine enter from the menagerie, with Rajah behind her. "How dare you!" she said. "Standing around, deciding my future. I am not a prize to be won!" Then she turned and stormed out.

Aladdin's heart sank. He had been sure she'd like him as a prince. He had never thought *this* would happen.

"Don't worry, Prince Ali," the Sultan said. "Just give her time to cool down. She'll warm to you."

Jafar watched silently as Aladdin and the Sultan walked into the menagerie. When they had gone, he turned to Iago and said. "It's time to say bye-bye to Prince Abooboo!"

CHAPTER NINE

Aladdin waited in the menagerie for the rest of the day. Jasmine's room was just overhead, but she refused to come to her balcony.

As night fell, Aladdin began to give up hope. "What am I going to do?" he moaned. "I should have known I couldn't pull off this stupid prince act."

Abu looked at his master and swung his trunk in sympathy.

"All right," the Genie said, looking up from a game of chess with the carpet. "Here's the deal. If you want to court her, you have to tell her the truth. Just be yourself!"

"No way!" said Aladdin. "If Jasmine found out I was really some crummy street rat, she'd laugh at me." He looked up at Jasmine's balcony and drew himself up straight. "I'm going to go and see her," he said. "I've got to be smooth. Cool. Confident."

The Genie sighed. He knew Aladdin was in for trouble.

The carpet slid beneath Aladdin and lifted him up to Jasmine's balcony. Through her window, Aladdin could see the Princess playing with Rajah. "Princess Jasmine?" he called out.

Jasmine turned and walked to the window. "Who's there?"

"It's me," said Aladdin. Then, remembering his Prince Ali voice, he added, "Prince Ali Ababwa."

"I do not want to see you!" Jasmine snapped.

As she turned away, Aladdin stepped off the carpet and onto the balcony. "Please, Princess, give me a chance!"

Rajah leapt into his path. Aladdin jerked away, almost losing his turban.

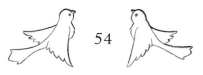

Jasmine narrowed her eyes. "Wait. Do I know you?" she asked. "You remind me of someone I met in the marketplace."

Aladdin backed into the shadows. "The marketplace? Why, I have *servants* who go to the marketplace for me! So it couldn't have been me you met."

"No, I guess not," Jasmine said, looking disappointed.

A bee buzzed by Aladdin's ear. He moved to swat it until he heard it speak—in the Genie's voice! "Enough about you," he said. "Talk about *her*!"

"Princess Jasmine, you're—uh, beautiful," Aladdin said.

"Rich, too," she said. "And the daughter of the Sultan."

Aladdin smiled. "I know."

"A fine prize for any prince to marry," she said, playing along.

"Right! A prince like me!"

"Right! A prince like you!" Jasmine repeated. "And every other swaggering peacock I've ever met. Go and jump off a balcony!" She turned and strode into her chamber.

"Mayday! Mayday!" said the Genie, still disguised as a bee. "Stop her! Want me to sting her?"

"Buzz off!" Aladdin replied.

"Okay," the Genie said. "But remember—*bee* yourself!"

"Yeah, right," Aladdin muttered as the Genie flew under his turban and into the lamp.

Jasmine looked over her shoulder. "What?"

"Uh… I said, you're *right*!" Aladdin sighed. "You… aren't just some prize to be won. You should be free to make your own choice."

Dejected, Aladdin turned away. He climbed over the railing and stepped off the balcony into space.

"No!" Jasmine cried. But Aladdin didn't fall – he was hovering in midair.

"How are you doing that?" Jasmine asked, stunned.

"It's a magic carpet," Aladdin replied.

Jasmine looked over the railing and touched the carpet. "It's lovely," she said softly.

"You don't want to go for a ride, do you?" Aladdin asked hopefully. "We could fly away and see the world."

"Is it safe?" Jasmine asked.

"Sure," said Aladdin. He held out his hand and smiled. "Do you trust me?"

Do you trust me? Jasmine had heard those exact words before, said in the same way. "Yes," she said, taking his hand and stepping onto the carpet.

As the carpet took off, she lost her balance and fell into Aladdin's arms. He blushed, but he liked the feeling – and he could tell that Jasmine did, too.

The carpet soared over the palace. Agrabah stretched out below them, a cluster of twinkling lights. Above them the stars of the desert sky winked as the couple glided over the sands. In the distance, the sea seemed to be made of the blackest ink.

Swooping among the pyramids, Aladdin and Jasmine whooped with joy. When the carpet flew through an orchard, Aladdin reached out and grabbed an apple for the Princess. He flipped it to her with a lopsided smile.

Jasmine smiled back. The casual flip; the smile; *Do you trust me?* – all of it was so much like the boy in the marketplace. Was it possible?

She decided to find out.

The carpet finally set them down on the roof of a tall pagoda, and they watched a fireworks display in the distance. "It's all so… magical," Jasmine said. "It's a shame Abu had to miss this."

"Nah," Aladdin said. "He hates fireworks. He doesn't really like to fly…"

Aladdin caught himself in mid-sentence.

"It *is* you!" Jasmine blurted. "Why did you lie to me? Did you think I wouldn't figure it out?"

"No! I mean, I *hoped* you wouldn't… no, that's not what I meant…" Aladdin groped for words. His stomach churned. He *couldn't* let Jasmine know the truth. "Um… the truth is, I sometimes dress as a commoner, to escape the pressures of palace life. But I really am Prince Ali Ababwa!"

Jasmine looked uncertain. "Why didn't you just tell me?"

"Well, you know… royalty going into the city in disguise… sounds a little strange, don't you think?"

Perfect! He knew he had her now. After all, *she* had been in disguise when he met her.

"Not that strange," she said, resting her chin on Aladdin's shoulder.

Together they watched the fireworks until they were too tired to keep their eyes open. The carpet then flew them back to the palace, hovering outside Jasmine's window.

Jasmine stepped onto the balcony, then turned towards Aladdin. They smiled at each other over the railing—until the carpet gave Aladdin a gentle nudge forward.

His lips suddenly met hers. She didn't move. In the soft light of the stars, they shared a long kiss.

"Good night, my handsome prince," she said, backing into her chamber.

"Sleep well, Princess," Aladdin replied.

As she disappeared behind a curtain, Aladdin grinned. "For the first time in my life," he murmured dreamily as the carpet floated down to the garden, "things are starting to go right."

He snapped back to reality when he felt the hard grip of rough hands on his shoulder. Turning round, Aladdin came face to face with Rasoul.

Before Aladdin could move, another guard slapped chains on his wrists and ankles. Rasoul stuffed a gag in his mouth.

"Abu!" Aladdin tried to yell through the gag. "Abu, help!"

He looked around wildly until he spotted Abu – hanging from a tree, tied up with thick rope. The carpet tried to fly away, but another guard threw it into a cage.

Jafar emerged from the shadows. On his shoulder, Iago was grinning. "I'm afraid you've worn out your welcome, Prince Abooboo," Jafar hissed.

Aladdin struggled against his chains. If only he could reach his turban. The lamp was under it – and the Genie was inside the lamp.

Jafar looked calmly at the guards. "Make sure he is never found."

CHAPTER TEN

In the chill of the desert night, the guards rushed Aladdin to the sea by camel. And without a word, they pushed him over a cliff.

Aladdin fell into the water with a loud splash. In the dim moonlight, he could see his turban floating away. The lamp slowly emerged, then dropped to the bottom of the sea.

Aladdin kicked, desperate to reach the lamp. He groped with his hands... There – he had it. But his strength was leaving him. He tried to rub the lamp, but he was weak... so weak...

SPLOOSH! The Genie materialized, wearing a shower cap and holding a brush. "Never fails," he said. "You get in the bath, and there's a rub at the lamp. Hello?"

Instantly his smile disappeared. Aladdin was drowning.

"Al! Kid! Snap out of it!" the Genie pleaded, grabbing Aladdin. "I can't help you unless you make a wish. You have to say, *Genie, I want you to save my life!* Got it?"

Aladdin's head bobbed ever so slightly.

"I'll take that as a yes!" The Genie let go of Aladdin and swam in a circle. A whirlpool formed, spinning Aladdin upwards.

He burst through the surface, coughing and flailing. Before he could fall, the Genie scooped Aladdin up and flew away. "Don't scare me like that!" he scolded.

Aladdin looked round with excitement. He was alive! As they flew back towards Agrabah, he looked into the smiling face of his rescuer.

"Genie, I... thanks," was all he could say.

At the palace, Jasmine was singing to herself as she got ready for bed.

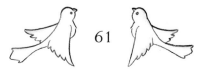

She had never been happier, and she couldn't stop thinking about her prince. She didn't notice her father walk in, followed by Jafar.

"Jasmine…" the Sultan began.

She whirled round. "Oh, Father!" she exclaimed. "I've just had the most wonderful time! I'm so happy!"

The Sultan stared straight ahead. "You should be, Jasmine," he said in a dull voice. "I have chosen a husband for you. You will marry Jafar."

Jafar stepped forward. The snake's head on his staff glowed brightly, working its hypnotic spell on the Sultan.

"Never!" Jasmine gasped. "Father, I choose Prince Ali!"

Jafar laughed. "Prince Ali left, like all the others. But don't worry. Wherever he went, I'm sure he made quite a *splash*."

"Better check your crystal ball, Jafar," came a voice from the window.

Jafar turned. Iago squawked in surprise. It was Aladdin!

Jasmine ran to him. "Prince Ali!" she cried. "Are you all right?"

"Yes," Aladdin said, "but no thanks to Jafar. He tried to have me killed!"

"Your Highness," said Jafar, "he's obviously lying."

"Obviously… lying…" repeated the Sultan mechanically.

"Father, what's wrong with you?" Jasmine said with dismay.

"I know what's wrong!" shouted Aladdin, leaping across to Jafar. He grabbed the staff and smashed the snake's head on the floor.

"Oh! Oh my…" the Sultan said, shaking his head. "I feel so strange."

"Your Highness," said Aladdin, holding the broken staff in the air, "Jafar's been controlling you with this!"

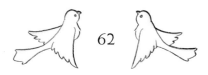

The Sultan's eyes narrowed. "You – you traitor!" he snapped at Jafar. "Guards! Arrest that man at once!"

But Jafar had caught sight of something he hadn't noticed before – peeping out of Aladdin's turban was the magic lamp! He lunged for it, but the Sultan's guards seized him.

"I'm not finished yet, boy!" said Jafar. Reaching into his robe, he pulled out a magic pellet and threw it on the floor. In a puff of smoke, he and Iago were gone.

"Find him!" the Sultan yelled to his guards. "I can't believe it – Jafar, my trusted counsellor, plotting against me!"

His shocked expression changed to a smile when he turned back to Jasmine and Aladdin. "Can it be? My daughter has finally chosen a suitor?"

Jasmine nodded, and the Sultan threw his arms round Aladdin. "Oh, you brilliant boy! You two will be married at once! You'll be happy, prosperous – and then you, my boy, will become Sultan!"

Sultan? Aladdin swallowed nervously. This was supposed to be the happiest moment of his life, but suddenly he was very worried.

ᑌᕋ◦ᑌᕋ

Iago flew round Jafar's laboratory in a blind panic. "We've got to get out of here!" he said. "I've got to pack!"

But Jafar was deep in thought. Suddenly he burst out laughing. "Of course," he exclaimed. "Prince Ali is nothing more than that ragged urchin Aladdin!" he said. "He has the *lamp*, Iago!"

"Why, that little cheating…" squawked Iago.

"But *you* are going to relieve him of it!" Jafar said with a sinister grin. "Listen closely." And he whispered his plan to Iago.

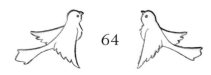

CHAPTER ELEVEN

Aladdin was given the most comfortable room in the palace that night, but he barely slept.

By dawn he was pacing back and forth, holding his turban, with the lamp inside. Abu and the carpet sat outside by the window, watching him with concern.

"*Huzzah!*" the Genie cried, popping out of the lamp. "Aladdin, you've just won the heart of the Princess! What are you going to do next?" He lowered his voice to a whisper. "Psst. Your next line is, *I'm going to free the Genie!*"

"Genie," Aladdin said sadly, "I'm sorry, but I can't. They want to make me Sultan—no, they want to make *Prince Ali* Sultan. The only reason anyone thinks I'm worth anything is because of you! What if they find out the truth? What if Jasmine finds out? She'll hate me." Aladdin looked into the Genie's disappointed face. "Genie, I need you. Without you, I'm just Aladdin."

The Genie tried to control his anger. "I understand. After all, you've lied to everyone else. Hey, I was beginning to feel left out. Now, if you'll excuse me!"

And he disappeared into the lamp.

"Genie!" Aladdin called out. "I'm really sorry."

The Genie stuck his tongue out of the spout at Aladdin and disappeared once more.

"Fine!" Aladdin snapped, throwing a pillow over the lamp. "Just stay in there!" As he stormed away, he could see Abu and the carpet watching him from the window. "What are you guys looking at?"

As Abu and the carpet turned away, Jasmine's voice came from the menagerie. "Ali? Will you please come here? Hurry!"

"Coming, Jasmine!" Aladdin called, rushing outside.

As he ran to the menagerie, Aladdin passed a group of flamingos in a pond.

At least, they all *looked* like flamingos.

Iago sniggered to himself. His imitation of Jasmine's voice had worked – and his flamingo disguise was perfect, thanks to Jafar's magic. When Aladdin had gone, Iago hurried into the empty room. In a flash, he had stolen the lamp and was winging his way back to Jafar's laboratory.

ᥬ ∘ ᥬ

"Ali! There you are," said Jasmine. "I've been looking all over for you!"

Aladdin looked round, puzzled. Jasmine was running towards him. But how could she have been *looking all over* when she had just...

"Hurry," she said, taking him by the hand. "Father's about to make the wedding announcement."

They climbed the stairs of a tower. Townspeople packed the courtyard, trying desperately to catch a glimpse of the royal couple. Jasmine stepped onto the platform and took her place next to her father. Smiling, the Sultan announced to the crowd, "Ladies and gentlemen, my daughter has chosen a suitor – Prince Ali Ababwa!"

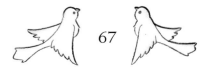

CHAPTER TWELVE

*H*igh in another tower, Jafar and Iago watched as Aladdin was about to step before the roaring crowd.

"Look at them cheering that pip-squeak," snorted Iago.

"Let them cheer," Jafar said as he rubbed the lamp. "At last," he continued, "the power is mine!"

In a puff of smoke, the Genie appeared. "Al, if you're going to apologize…" The Genie's jaw dropped when he saw Jafar.

"*I* am your master now!" Jafar said.

"I was afraid of that."

"Keep quiet!" snapped Jafar. "And now, slave, grant me my first wish. I wish to be Sultan!"

 ❦

As Aladdin stared down from the platform, the crowd suddenly became hazy. Clouds swirled over the palace, and with a loud tearing sound, the canopy over the platform was ripped off. Jasmine and Aladdin looked round in confusion as a strange magical light engulfed the Sultan. When it stopped, the Sultan was on the floor – in his underwear! The crowd gasped.

There was someone else on the platform now – someone tall, dark and dressed in the Sultan's robes. He held a snake's head staff in his right hand.

"Jafar!" Aladdin exclaimed.

Jafar turned with a sneer. "*Sultan* Jafar to you!"

"What manner of trickery is this?" the Sultan demanded.

"Finders keepers," Jafar said. "I have the ultimate power now!"

A shadow fell over the courtyard. Everyone looked up.

Looming over them like an evil giant was the Genie. He put his hands on the palace as if he were about to crush it.

"Genie, stop!" Aladdin shouted. "What are you doing?"

"Sorry, kid," said the Genie sadly. "I've got a new master now."

With a mighty heave, he lifted the entire palace off the ground. The Genie flew to a mountain high above the city and set the palace down there.

Jafar let out a deep, triumphant laugh, and whirled round to face the Genie. "My second wish is to be the most powerful sorcerer in the world!"

His staff began to glow, and green lightning crackled around it. Rajah let out a roar and lunged at him. Jafar waved his staff and, in midair, Rajah was transformed into a kitten.

Jafar turned to Jasmine next. "Now," he said, with a vicious gleam in his eye, "take a look at your precious Prince Ali – or should we say *Aladdin?*"

A bolt of light shot from his staff and surrounded Aladdin and Abu. Instantly Abu became a monkey again. Aladdin's cloak, silk shirt and turban disappeared. He fell to the floor, dressed in his old rags. "He's nothing more than a worthless, lying street rat!" shouted Jafar.

Jasmine looked at Aladdin, confused and hurt. "Ali?" she said.

"Jasmine… I'm sorry," said Aladdin.

Jafar waved his staff again, and Aladdin and Abu suddenly rose off the ground and were carried through the open window of a narrow tower. In an instant, the tower rocketed over the horizon. The carpet sped after it.

And as the tower disappeared, Jafar shouted, "At last! Agrabah is mine!"

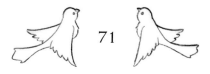

71

CHAPTER THIRTEEN

When Aladdin awoke he was cold—freezing cold. As he made his way out of a snowbank, an icy wind whipped more snow into his face.

Where was he? Through the raging blizzard, he could see the tower lying in pieces, half covered with snow. Just beyond it, a cliff plunged downwards into darkness.

A crash—that was all he remembered. He must have been thrown out of the tower, unconscious.

Something in the snow caught his attention. "Abu!" he called through chattering teeth. He raced over and dug the monkey out. "Are you all right?"

Shivering, Abu nodded weakly.

Aladdin tucked Abu into his waistcoat. "Oh, Abu, this is all my fault," he said. "I should have freed the Genie when I had the chance. Somehow, I've got to go back and set things straight."

He felt something tickling his leg. Spinning round, he looked down and saw the carpet reaching towards him. It was caught beneath a huge chunk of the tower.

Aladdin tried to pull the carpet free, but it was stuck tight. He and Abu started digging a trench. Then, suddenly, the tower began to wobble.

"Look out!" Aladdin shouted, as the tower started rolling towards them.

Aladdin ducked, enfolding Abu in his arms. The tower rolled right over them, somehow leaving them unharmed. They watched as it plunged over the cliff.

Freed from the tower, the carpet scooped up Aladdin and Abu and rose above the clouds.

"All right!" cried Aladdin. "Now, back to Agrabah!"

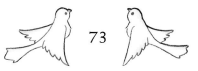

Jafar loved the view from his new throne room. The palace was where it belonged now—on a mountain top, not in the midst of the rabble. He sipped happily from his wineglass as the Genie massaged his feet. The *former* Sultan was now suspended from the ceiling like a puppet. He was dressed in a jester's outfit, and Jafar and Iago sneered at the ridiculous sight. Rajah, still a kitten, paced anxiously in a cage.

Jasmine sat at the window, her wrists in shackles, her eyes filled with sadness.

Jafar reached out with his staff and pulled her close to him. "It pains me to see you like this, Jasmine," he said. "You should be by the side of the most powerful man in the world." With a wave of the staff, he made the chains vanish. A crown appeared on her head. "Why, with you as my queen…"

Jasmine took his glass and threw the wine in his face. "Never!"

Jafar bolted out of the throne. "Temper, temper, Jasmine," he scolded. "You know what happens when you misbehave. I'll teach you some respect!" He glared at the Genie. "Genie, I have decided to make my final wish—I wish that Princess Jasmine would fall desperately in love with me!"

"No!" cried Jasmine, backing away.

"But, Master," the Genie said, "I can't do that!"

"You will do whatever I order you to do, slave!" roared Jafar as he grabbed the Genie's beard.

Nobody noticed Aladdin and Abu at the throne room window—nobody except Jasmine. She opened her mouth, but Aladdin signalled to her not to say anything. Then he, Abu and the carpet climbed silently into the room.

Jasmine thought quickly. "Jafar," she said with a seductive smile, "I never realized how incredibly handsome you are!"

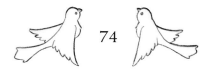

Jafar spun round. His jaw hung open in disbelief—and so did the Genie's.

"That's better," Jafar said. He slunk towards Jasmine, a cocky smile on his face. "Now, tell me more about... *myself*."

"You're tall, dark..." Jasmine could see Aladdin, Abu and the carpet sneaking towards the lamp. Then the Genie saw them, too, and tried to stifle an excited giggle.

"Go on..." Jafar demanded.

Abu was very close to Iago now—and Iago was turning round. Jasmine swiftly put her arms round Jafar, locking him in place. "You're well dressed," she continued. "You've stolen my heart..."

With a quick leap, Abu grabbed Iago off his perch and put a paw over his beak. They both tumbled to the ground.

"And the street rat?" Jafar said, drawing closer to Jasmine.

"*What* street rat?" Jasmine asked.

CRASSSHHH! Abu and Iago knocked into a table, sending a pot to the ground.

Jafar started to turn. Jasmine had no choice but to pull him close and kiss him—passionately.

Now was Aladdin's chance. But he couldn't move. All he could do was stare. There she was, the girl for whom he had risked his life, kissing... *him*.

Jafar pulled back. He was dazed with joy—until he saw Aladdin's reflection in Jasmine's crown.

"You!" he said, whirling round in blind rage and pointing his staff at Aladdin.

ZZZZZZZAP! A flash of light struck Aladdin in the chest. He flew backwards, crashing into a pile of jewels.

"How many times do I have to kill you, boy?" said Jafar, drawing his arm back for a second shot.

Jasmine leapt at him, pushing his arm aside.

"You deceiving shrew!" Jafar snarled. "Your time is up!"

He turned his staff on Jasmine. Instantly she was trapped inside a giant hourglass. The upper chamber was full of sand, which was slowly spilling through the opening onto her. There was more than enough to bury her alive.

ZZZZZAP! With a stroke of the staff, Jafar turned Abu into a cymbal-clanging toy monkey.

ZZZZZAP! The carpet began to unravel.

"This is all your fault, street rat!" Jafar shouted at Aladdin. "You never should have come back!" ZZZZZAP! A sword clattered to the ground beside Aladdin, then another. He looked up. Dozens of razor-sharp swords were falling from the ceiling.

Jafar pointed his staff again, and a wall of fire burst from the floor.

Aladdin grabbed one of the fallen swords. "Are you afraid to fight me yourself, you cowardly snake?" Aladdin challenged, batting away the swords as they fell.

Jafar made his way towards Aladdin, forcing him closer to the fire.

"A snake, am I? Perhaps you'd like to see how snakelike I can be!"

Jafar held out his snake staff with both hands. It began to grow, coming to hideous life, wrapping Jafar himself into its skin. Swelling, hissing, Jafar became a monstrous cobra, his head rising towards the ceiling. The flames rose with him, becoming a ring of deadly coils surrounding Aladdin.

With an unearthly roar, Jafar lunged. Aladdin swung his sword.

SHINK! He struck two of Jafar's fangs, which clattered onto the floor.

"*Rickum-rackum*, stick that sword into that snake," the Genie shouted.

"You stay out of this!" hissed Jafar. He lunged again, knocking Aladdin to the floor. The sword flew out of his hand.

"Ali!" the Sultan cried, watching helplessly from above. "*Jasmine!*"

In the hourglass, the sand was rising swiftly. It covered all but Jasmine's head.

Without his sword, Aladdin had only one chance. He ran for the window and leapt onto the balcony. Jafar slithered after him. Quickly Aladdin ran back in, then ducked out of another window.

Jafar followed from window to window, tangling his long body into a knot. He shrieked with pain.

Aladdin picked up his sword and ran towards the hourglass. Jasmine's nose was barely above the sand now, and her eyes were wide with fear. Aladdin drew back the sword, ready to smash the glass.

Suddenly, with a resounding boom, Jafar pulled down the wall. He was free—and he threw his coils round Aladdin.

"You thought you could outwit the most powerful being on earth?" bellowed Jafar.

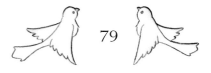

Aladdin wrenched left and right. In a corner of the room, the Genie watched helplessly.

The Genie!

Thinking quickly, Aladdin said, "You're not so powerful. The Genie has more power than you'll ever have! He gave you your power, and he can take it away!"

The Genie ducked behind a pillar. "Al, what are you doing? Why are you bringing me into this?"

"Face it, Jafar, you're still just second," Aladdin continued.

Jafar loosened his coils. He turned his evil face to the Genie. "You're right. His power does exceed my own—but not for long!"

Aladdin fell to the floor as Jafar slithered across the room. "Slave!" Jafar called to the Genie. "I'm ready to make my third wish. I wish to be—an all-powerful genie!"

The Genie looked at Aladdin, his blue face now chalk white. "Your wish," he said to Jafar in a small, wavering voice, "is my command!"

CHAPTER FOURTEEN

The Genie gestured. A swirling current of energy encircled Jafar, and he began to change shape. The fire disappeared. His cobra body became wider and wider until he took on the roundness of a genie. "Yes!" Jafar shrieked. "The power! The absolute power!"

Quickly Aladdin picked up his sword and smashed the hourglass. Jasmine slid forward with the cascading sand. "What have you done?" she asked as Aladdin pulled her free.

Aladdin smiled. "Trust me!"

"The universe is an open book before me!" Jafar yelled. "Mine to command, to control!" The dome of the palace exploded as Jafar rose towards the sky.

Before he could say another word, gold chains encircled his wrists – just like the ones the Genie wore. A lamp began to materialize beneath him, new and shiny.

"*Whaaat?* What is happening?" Jafar demanded.

"You wanted to be a genie?" said Aladdin, picking up the new lamp. Then he held it out to Jafar. "Well, you've got your wish – and everything that goes with it!"

Jafar's legs were now a trail of vapour disappearing into the lamp's spout. "No!" he screamed, his eyes bulging in terror. "*NOOOOOOO!*"

Squealing with anguish, Jafar reached up and grabbed Iago's feet. "Wha – hey! Let go!" cried Iago.

With a dull *THOOMP*, Jafar and Iago were sucked into the lamp.

Everyone in the throne room fell into an awed silence. Jasmine, the Sultan and the Genie stared at Aladdin.

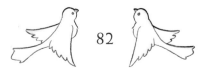

"Phenomenal cosmic powers," Aladdin said with a shrug, "itty-bitty living space!"

The Genie let out a loud cackle. "Al, you little genius!"

Instantly the room began to return to normal. Back on his feet, the Sultan sighed with pleasure as his robes materialized on him. Abu became a live monkey again. Rajah grew back into a tiger, breaking free of his small cage. And the carpet looked brand new.

The Genie grabbed the lamp and went to the balcony. "Shall we? Ten thousand years in the Cave of Wonders ought to chill him out!" And he hurled the lamp as hard as he could, sending it reeling towards the desert.

Smiling proudly, the Genie flew outside. He grew to a gigantic shape, picked up the palace, and carried it back to its rightful place.

CHAPTER FIFTEEN

*L*ater that day, when Agrabah had returned to normal, Jasmine and Aladdin stood on the throne room balcony.

"Jasmine," Aladdin said softly, "I'm sorry I lied to you... about being a prince."

Jasmine nodded. "I know why you did."

"I guess... this is goodbye?"

Jasmine turned away. "That stupid law! It isn't fair!" Slowly, tearfully, she faced Aladdin again. "I love you."

Suddenly the Genie popped through the window. "Al, no problem—you've got one wish left. Just say the word, and you're a prince again!"

"But Genie," Aladdin said. "What about your freedom?"

"Al, you're in love. You're not going to find another girl like this in a million years. Believe me, I've looked."

Aladdin looked from the Genie to Jasmine. He knew how much freedom meant now. Not only to the Genie but to Jasmine—and to himself. Just as she needed to be free of the Sultan's laws, Aladdin needed to be free, too. Free to be himself.

"Jasmine... I do love you," he finally said. "But I can't pretend to be something I'm not."

Jasmine bowed her head. "I understand."

"Genie," Aladdin said, "I wish for your freedom. It's about time I started keeping my promises."

In a flash, the Genie's gold cuffs vanished. He was stunned. "Quick! Wish for something—anything! Say, *I want the Nile!*"

"Er—I wish for the Nile," said Aladdin.

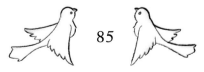

"*NO WAY!*" cried the Genie with a laugh. "I'm free!" he shouted, his face lighting up. "I'm free! I'm off to see the world!"

"Congratulations!" the Sultan said, peeping out from behind him.

"Genie, I'm going to miss you," Aladdin said.

"Me, too, Al," the Genie replied with a fond smile. "No matter what anybody says, you'll always be a prince to me!"

"That's right!" agreed the Sultan. "You've certainly proved your worth as far as I'm concerned. If it's the law that's the problem, then what we need is a new one!"

Jasmine looked at him, stunned. "Father?"

"From this day forth, the Princess shall marry whomever she deems worthy!"

"I choose you, Aladdin!" Jasmine cried instantly.

Aladdin was ecstatic. "Call me Al," he said.

He and Jasmine burst out laughing. Aladdin took her in his arms, and the two of them began twirling across the balcony.

"Well!" the Genie said with a huge smile. "I can't do any more damage in this place. And now I'm out of here! Bye-bye, you crazy lovebirds!"

Like a rocket, the Genie launched himself into the sky and disappeared over the horizon.

Aladdin and Jasmine didn't even notice him leave. As they shared a long, dreamy kiss, they hardly noticed anything at all – except each other.

THE END